Hotwife Tattoo - A Wife Watching Multiple Partner Hotwife Romance Novel

Karly Violet

Published by Karly Violet, 2021.

HOTWIFE TATTOO - A WIFE WATCHING MULTIPLE PARTNER HOTWIFE ROMANCE NOVEL

First edition. December 20, 2021.

Copyright © 2021 Karly Violet.

ISBN: 979-8201608163

Written by Karly Violet.

Hotel Tattoo

A Wife Watching Multiple Partner Hotwife Romance Novel

Note that this work of fiction resembles a fantasy world, all events taking place are a result of a role play amongst all parties and all parties are fully consenting adults.

Chapter One: Mystery Ink

"Well, good morning, sunshine!" I smile widely as I watch my wife walk sluggishly into the kitchen. It's late Saturday morning and Darla obviously had more than her share to drink last night while out with her friends.

"Not so loud," she mumbles as she leans against one of the counters. "My head is throbbing."

Shaking my head, I chuckle. "You're thirty years old, babe. You shouldn't be out like that all night. It's going to take its toll on you soon." I hold out a cup of black coffee and Darla takes it from me. She sniffs it and winces as she looks back at me.

"*Straight* coffee? Not even a little creamer, Leo?"

"Straight coffee, babe. You need it to help fight off the headache that you have right now. Caffeine is the name of the game." I watch as my wife slowly lifts the cup to her lips. She takes a sip and swallows before wincing once again as she takes a second sip. Darla knows she needs to get liquids down this morning. It's far too easy to get dehydrated after a night of heavy drinking.

"I've got to sit down." She turns and walks slowly to the kitchen table nearby and has a seat in one of the chairs.

"Wild party, huh?" I say as I have a seat next to her.

"I don't know," Darla giggles a little before putting her hand on her forehead. "Fuck. I need some Tylenol."

"Uh, no," I reply sternly. "Maybe a little aspirin, but no Tylenol or Advil. It's not safe after drinking so hard." I get back up and walk over to the cabinet where we keep a few medications. Reaching in, I retrieve a packet of BC Powder and take it to the table. "Here. Swallow this."

She shakes her head. "There's no fucking way I'm putting that powder into my mouth, Leo. That stuff is bitter as hell."

"Like the shots you were doing last night?" I laugh a little as I tease her. Though we both occasionally drink, I make it a point to never go on the sort of benders that Darla sometimes allows for herself. No, my days of getting hammered are long behind me.

"Shots. Oh, the shots." She grins a little. "Tequila. Lots and lots of tequila."

"Let me guess. Tess?"

"Tess is a rock star," Darla giggles as she opens up the BC Powder pack. "Oh, I don't think I can do this."

"It's the only thing we have that won't kill your liver right now, babe. If you want to manage that headache, you might want to just open your mouth and swallow."

Her green eyes turn to look into mine. "You just like it when I swallow, huh?"

I grin. "Of course I do, my love." Looking down at the floor as I turn my chair to face her, I see that my wife's ankle has a small bandage on it. "Did you hurt yourself last night?" I point to the dressing just above her ankle bone.

Darla looks down at it. "Oh. What's that?" She reaches down and touches it. "Ouch. Something hurts."

"You don't remember what you did that required a bandage? Babe, you need to be more careful. This drinking with your friends like this has got to stop." I kneel down into the floor and lift her foot. Gently peeling back the bandage, I'm shocked at what I find. "A *butterfly?*"

"What?" Darla backs her chair away from the table and puts her foot on her other knee. She finishes removing the white bandage and just stares at the tattoo on her ankle. "Where did that come from?"

"You honestly don't know?"

"No, I swear to it. I don't know how that got there." Her eyes grow wide as she pulls her shoulder-length blonde hair behind her ear. "I don't remember going to get a tattoo, Leo. Shit."

I shake my head. "Your friends must have taken you somewhere while you were hammered. You're lucky that they didn't get you pierced, too." I look at my wife's tee shirt and the nipples poking through the thin fabric.

Darla nearly panics as she lifts her shirt to reveal her round orbs and medium sized pink nipples. "Oh, fuck. Thank goodness they didn't do that to me." She puts her shirt down before focusing on her ankle again.

"You don't remember." I laugh. "How the hell, Darla? You can't do this anymore."

She pauses and thinks for a moment as she has another sip of coffee. "I remember something about butterflies, but it's just not clear to me what happened. How could I not have known that someone was putting that on me? It stings a little even now."

Shrugging my shoulders, I reply, "If you're fucking drunk, that kills a lot of the pain. I'm shocked that a tattoo parlor would even do that while you were so out of it."

"I might have been awake and seemed alert, Leo. You know how I can sometimes just black out after drinking but be able to hold a conversation."

"That's why you need to quit doing that, babe. One of these days you're going to do something really stupid. I mean, you could have even gotten a clit ring." I peer wickedly at her shorts and she laughs.

"I know what you're up to, Leo. No, I'm not taking off my shorts to look right now." We both laugh as she reaches over and runs her fingers through my dark brown hair. "You're right, though. That was dangerous. The tattoo could have been huge and ugly. At least this is cute and small." Darla looks at the colorful butterfly tattoo before asking, "What do you think?"

I smile. "Well, I've never really thought you to be the tattoo type, but here you are with a tattoo." Looking it over, I comment, "It's kind of sexy, though."

"Sexy?" Darla raises an eyebrow as she looks at me.

"In a good way," I laugh. "Not in a slutty way or anything like that." I stand up and then sit down in the chair beside my wife. "You probably went with them willingly, and just don't remember the tattoo parlor at all. I wonder if any of the others got a tattoo as well?"

Darla looks at me and nods. "Yeah, that would be an interesting question. I'll text some of them in a while once my headache is a little better." She takes another sip of the black coffee and then puts the cup on the table. "I think it was a game. The shots of tequila, that is. Some kind of game where we were constantly taking more shots. I wish I could remember it all."

"Like I said before, you're thirty years old now. It's time for you to stop going out and partying like that with Tess and the rest of them. Some of them already have children."

"And I don't." A somber expression fills my wife's face. I've said the wrong thing and I wish I could take it back.

"I don't mean it like that. All of you are too old to be acting as if you're still in college."

"But I don't have kids. That's on me, right?" Darla huffs as she crosses her arms. We found out just last year that my wife's ovaries aren't producing viable eggs for the most part. I had hoped that the problem would end up being with me and we could just borrow some sperm, but instead it was discovered that she can't give her half of the DNA needed for a child.

"It's not on you." I reach out and take her hand. Darla is shaking as she looks into my eyes. "Remember, we've talked about this, babe. You can't help what's been dealt to you. We're fine the way we are. I don't feel like we need kids."

"But we do, Leo. Eventually. What then?"

"Maybe adopt?" I squeeze her hands. "Don't let this bother you, Darla. We will have children when we're ready, alright? They might not be biologically ours, but they *will* be *ours.*" After pulling some of her blonde hair from her face, I tell my wife, "But the drinking all night has got to come to an end. You can't come home like you did early this morning with a tattoo on your ankle that you don't remember getting. The next time it could be an Elmer Fudd tattoo on your chest. Or a giant penis on your forehead." We both laugh and embrace each other. I love

Darla very much and I don't like to see her upset. I'm also concerned that she feels like going out all night with friends is the answer for her when it's obviously not.

"I love you, Leo," she says before kissing me on the cheek. Darla finishes up her cup of coffee as well as the BC Powder in front of her before getting up and leaving the kitchen. I watch as she makes her way to the bedroom and likely to the bathroom where she'll have a quick shower. She needs it. She still smells of the strong drink that has given her a hangover.

"Oh, babe. I wish you would give this lifestyle up. It's just not you anymore. It's not either of us." I get up from my chair and collect the empty powder packet and the coffee cup. After putting them in their proper places, I go to the bedroom to get dressed to go into the city. Darla arrived in an Uber last night, which means that her car is still at the bar. I need to collect it and get it back to the house before it gets towed. This isn't the first time I've had to do this. It will likely not be the last.

Chapter Two: A Wild Wife

There are times in our investment firm when things get a little boring around here. Today, for example, I have only spoken to three clients. It's a slow trading and investing day, so one of my colleagues in the office, Justin Cole, decides to sit down on the edge of my desk to visit with me.

"So, um, how's your client list coming along?" he asks with a smirk.

I look up at him. "Better than yours."

"Really? I've found one new client this morning already. He's coming in this afternoon to fill out the paperwork."

"Okay. You have me beat there. I'm just talking to current clients for now," I answer as I roll my chair back away from my desk so that I can look at him without straining my neck. "You had better not get caught sitting on a desk if Mike comes by."

"Mike, schmike," Justin says with a grin. "He's probably back in his office jerking off to a dirty magazine or something."

"Internet website. Nobody buys the paper copies anymore." We both laugh as I shake my head. "Darla came home this weekend with a tattoo that she can't remember getting," I offer as I change the topic. I don't know why I would share this sort of thing with Justin, but we've worked together for more than three years now and I feel like I can tell him just about anything.

"Really? Where at?"

"Her ankle. It's a small butterfly."

"How does it look?" Justin smiles widely at me.

"It's sexy," I admit while allowing my own smile to cross my face. "But she did it without remembering doing it. She was out drunk with some of her friends."

"Ah, she likes doing that, right?" I nod my head. "Some ladies do. You and I could as well, if you were of the mind to go out once in a decade."

"Justin, you know that I don't do that. I mean, I did in college and for a while once I got out, but there's really no reason for me to go out and get drunk now. I hate the feeling of being hungover the next morning."

"Hey, nobody likes that, but you have to admit that it's sometimes worth it to have the adventure." Justin is the sort of guy who enjoys his whiskey. As a matter of fact, there's a small bottle stashed inside his desk drawer right now, and if our manager Mike Greenwald ever found out about it, Justin would probably lose his job.

"It's not worth the puking and ringing in the ears. I don't mind a drink or two occasionally, but I don't get sloshed."

"And she was sloshed?"

"Completely. Darla came home and changed before dropping into bed. Her breath still smelled like an open bottle of Jack Daniels, too." I shake my head. "She's an elementary school teacher. If she keeps this up, it might affect her work and they would fire her for that."

"I see." Justin nods his head before leaning over and saying quietly, "You should just let her do it, man. Let Darla be who she wants to be, no matter the consequences. I mean, I did that with Becky back in the day."

"Becky. Your ex-wife? *That* Becky?" I snort as I chuckle.

"She was happy with me as long as I let her do what she wanted. The woman was wild and I needed to let her be free."

"That wild woman you were married to felt free to have an affair behind your back, Justin. Have you forgotten about that?"

My colleague recoils a little. "Sure she did, but we had a good marriage overall."

"A good marriage doesn't end because one of the people in it starts poking someone else on the side." I shake my head. "No, I don't plan to tell Darla to just party like it's a normal thing. She's in the public eye enough that she could lose her job. Besides, she's too old to behave like a college kid."

"She's an adult," Justin reminds me. "She can do whatever she wants when she's off and having a good time with her friends. Leo, you should just let the woman do it if she wants to do it. She'll love you for it. Maybe she'll come home with another tattoo to show off."

I laugh. "Yeah, like a giant nude woman on her chest or a Santa Claus tattoo on her ass. No thanks. This could have been much worse than it was." As a matter of fact, I had a nightmare last night in which Darla had gotten a tattoo of some other man on her lower leg. She had decided to run off with him and leave me. I awoke with sweat all over my body and my heart racing.

"Then go with her to get a tattoo. Maybe if you help to ink the lady up she'll be less likely to visit a tattoo joint later on with her friends." Justin smiles. "Maybe get her a tramp stamp on her lower back."

"Seriously? Is that what they call that?"

"It makes for entertainment when having doggystyle sex with your lady." Justin moves his hands around in front of him as if he's guiding a woman's ass toward his crotch while having sex with her. "Just keep an open mind, my friend. Ladies love ink."

"Well, I'm not getting anything on me and I'm definitely not encouraging her to do something else. I'm worried as to what she might want."

"She might want a tattoo of fuzzy dice on her tits." Justin laughs as I begin to wonder whether he's been taking sips from his whiskey bottle this morning.

"No, I'm not going to tell her to get any more tattoos or to go out and drink with her friends. Things need to change for her. She's a teacher, after all. Not a prostitute."

Just now, Mike walks by and stops in front of my desk. "What the hell is your ass doing on that desk, Justin?"

He hops up and looks at our manager. "Mike. Fancy meeting you here."

The manager shakes his head. "Just keep your cheeks off the desktops and get back to work." Mike looks down at me. "Both of you." He then turns and continues to walk down the corridor toward the breakroom.

"Miserable old fart," Justin jokes as he sits back down on the top of my desk. "I wonder if he's had his bowel movement today?"

"Come on, Justin. We need to get back to work."

"He probably needs a few stewed prunes to get himself going again."

"Justin."

"Oh, alright." He stands up and chuckles. "Just talk to her about having some clean fun with you instead of her friends. You could even promise to take her for a small, tasteful tattoo. Darla would probably like that, Leo. Try it out and see what happens."

I nod my head. "I'll think about it." Justin gets up and leaves my office as I begin to think about what he's suggested. "She doesn't need another one," I say to myself. "And, she probably doesn't want one. Those other ladies took her to the tattoo parlor while she was too drunk to know better." My cell phone buzzes and I pick it up. My wife is texting me.

"How is your day?" She follows this with a pair of kissing lips emoji.

"Good. Yours?"

"Busy. In meetings all day. Kids aren't here." I had forgotten that today there is no school for students, only the teachers and staff are on campus at her school. Darla is there learning something else that the department of education apparently feels their teachers need to know.

"Feeling okay?" I don't know why I send this. I suppose I feel that she might still be affected by Friday night's imbibement.

"I'm okay. Why?" She sends an emoji with a raised eyebrow and monocle.

"No reason, babe. I just like to know that all is well with you. We should go out or something this weekend. Just me and you and none of your friends. How does that sound?" I send the text message and simply wait for a response. Over the last four weekends, I haven't spent a single Friday evening with Darla. Instead, she has opted to go out with her friends. This needs to stop.

"I guess we could. Saturday?"

"Saturday morning," I tell her. "And you don't go out the night before." I send it and nervously await her response.

"Leo, I won't do it again. I promise. I want to see Renee for dinner and talk for a while."

"And drink," I retort. "You are always going out to drink. Why not stay home this time and then spend the next morning with me?" I get why she doesn't want to spend a lot of time with me. It has a lot to do with the fact that we can't have a baby together. Ever since we received this news six months ago, my wife has been slow to willingly enjoy much time with just me in our bedroom. It's as if our sex life has lost some of its spice.

"Just trust me, alright?" There are three other emojis with various sorts of smiles that come through the text message. Darla has come to rely on her friends. So, I should just be okay with her doing that, right?

"Fine. But you're mine on Saturday and I don't want you drunk or hungover. Deal?"

She sends a smiling emoji again. "Deal! I love you, sweetie!"

"I love you too." I shake my head as I put my phone down on the desktop in front of me. Darla means the world to me and I hate that such bad news about her fertility has caused her so much pain. When the doctor came into the room to deliver the news, she was so somber. My wife began to cry before the doctor could even say what was wrong. Darla already knew. I think she has always known somehow.

"Don't forget about James Downs," I hear someone say before I lift my head to look at who is speaking. The investment firm manager looks hard at me as he reminds me about one of my best clients. "Since things are a little off today, he would be a good one to call. There might be some extra money lying around somewhere that he wouldn't mind investing in a good portfolio, Leo. Give him a ring and find out." Mike then turns and walks away without saying another word.

It's never, "Hello, how's your day," with the manager. He's a nice enough guy, but while at work he's all-business. I get that, especially considering that we all work primarily on commission. If we don't get more clients or at least invest our clients' money in a responsible way, we don't get paid. So, it behooves us all to try to get current clients to dig themselves even deeper into our managed portfolios if we can. It just so happens that James Downs has already agreed to invest another hundred thousand just this morning after I spoke with him on the phone. Even so, my mind continues to move toward my wife and her desires.

"Just be careful. Be an adult," I say quietly to myself as I think about Darla and her wish to go out with a friend on Friday night. "Stay away from the tequila shots." I smile to myself as I think about that little tattoo on her ankle. A part of me wishes that my wife had gotten a clit ring as well. That would have been something to see and to play with!

Chapter Three: Her Body the Canvas

15

We walk along the sidewalk as Darla pulls close to me while holding my hand. "Come on, tell me what you're doing," she says as she giggles.

I smile. "It's a surprise. A friend gave me an idea the other day and I want to see what you think about it." It's hard to keep my mouth shut about something whenever Darla asks me. She has the uncanny ability to pull secrets out of me as if she's sucking the jism right out of my balls. Though I want to tell her, I won't. I want to see the surprise on her face when we finally arrive.

"Aren't you proud of me, Leo? I came home totally sober last night."

I chuckle. "You behaved like an adult woman. Yes, I'm very proud." The truth be known, I waited up for my wife until midnight and very much thought that she would walk through the door totally inebriated. However, she was as sober and clear minded as anyone could be. According to her, she didn't have anything other than water to drink with her friend last night. I'm not sure I believe her to that extent, but it was definitely nice to see her come home in good shape.

"What's this?" she asks as we stop in front of a large tattoo shop.

"This is where we are going," I tell her before leading my wife inside through the door.

"Hello!" A young woman with two fully inked sleeves and a bullring in her nose smiles as she approaches us. "What can I help you both with today?"

"Leo," Darla whispers as she looks at me from the side.

"We're here to look over some of your tattoo designs. My wife and I might be wanting to get something nice for ourselves."

The woman nods her head. "Oh? What sort of art are you looking for?"

"Leo," Darla says again, this time a little louder.

I turn to look at her and chuckle a little as I reply, "What?"

"You've made your point." My wife looks nervously at the tattooed woman. "I'm really sorry about this. My husband is being a bit of a dick right now."

The woman smiles. "We get a lot of those in here."

"It's this." Darla points toward her ankle tattoo of a butterfly.

"Cute. It's not really our thing here, though." The woman looks at me. "Let me guess. You want one too?"

"Uh, no," I say with a laugh. "I just thought that maybe we could consider something a little more substantial than the butterfly that she has. Something that others would actually look at and be amazed to see when she shows it off."

"Seriously?" My wife seems shocked that I would actually want her to get another tattoo. It's not the sort of thing that I've talked about wanting to do myself, but I've given it some thought. Maybe we should both get a little more ink on ourselves.

"We have some very nice designs," the woman replies, before adding, "By the way, I'm Sheila." She offers her hand and I shake it. My cock stiffens a little as I imagine the young woman riding me in bed, her tattoos in motion as she kisses me, her bull ring gently scraping my cheek.

"I'm Leo and this is Darla," I reply. The women shake hands.

"Have a seat." Sheila points toward a very nice pair of leather seats. We sit down and she reaches for a large book before laying it down on the table in front of us. "So, why a butterfly?" she asks as she looks at my wife.

Darla blushes a little as she shrugs her shoulders. "I didn't really plan to do that. It just happened." She looks at me, probably worried that I might say something about how she acquired the lepidopteran's visage on her ankle.

"Drunk, huh?" Sheila answers knowingly with a smile. "We get a few of those in here. We turn them away, though. Plus, we don't do butterflies, unicorns, or rainbows here." She looks at us. "Each piece of art has a separate price. Let me know if you see something that you like and we'll talk about it." We begin to turn the pages to look at the intricate work that the tattoo shop offers. The artwork ranges from the simple, yet elegant, to the colorful and very intricate. I assume that the more work put into the tattoo, the greater the cost. That doesn't matter to me, though. I want to see something sexy on Darla.

"This one," I say as I point to one piece of art that is long, black, and flowing. "That's an interesting one."

Sheila nods her head. "That's one that I've done a couple of times. Both times have been women. It means to be sexually healthy and fertile."

"Fertile?" Darla shrinks back into her chair. "There's nothing fertile about me."

"Babe, it's just something that people might think that it means if they've seen it before. Most people haven't seen this tattoo. I've never seen it."

"And like I've already said, I've only done two so far. It's not all that common, which lends to the coolness of the work." Sheila smiles. She obviously likes the way the curved lines in the artwork move around each other as they go from one end to the other.

"Where would it normally go?" Darla asks.

"The arm or back. Possibly the leg," she replies. "It's a longer piece, so you don't want to limit the canvas if at all possible. It just wouldn't look as stunning."

"I see." My wife moves her fingers along the lines in the image as she considers the tattoo. "The back?"

Sheila nods. "From the base of your neck to your tailbone would be very attractive. You could even wear a backless dress to show it off if you would like."

"I've seen women do that before," I reply. "I think it's really sexy."

"And it means to be fertile," Darla interjects. "It's a lie."

"It's a *hope,*" I tell her. "The doctor said it might be possible that you'll be able to get pregnant one day."

"A five percent chance," my wife responds dryly. "And yet, I'm going to advertise that I'm a fertile woman."

"There are many ways to be fertile as a woman," Sheila interrupts. "A woman can be sensual and giving. Isn't that a form of fertility? She can be intelligent and well-versed in important things. I believe that's a form of fertility as well. Don't limit yourself. You get to pick what your art will be. No one else can force you to be what you don't want to be, and you can decide what you will ultimately become."

I'm impressed to hear the sage advice from the young tattoo artist. Honestly, I thought that we would encounter some middle-aged chubby guy with a beard who would want to put an even larger butterfly with skulls and crossbones on Darla's chest. Sheila, though, seems to have her shit together. It causes my confidence in her as an artist to rise.

"I think you should do it," I tell Darla. "Sheila's right. You make things what you want them to be. You define yourself. If you want it, you've got it."

"And the cost?"

"Don't worry about it," I say to my wife. "I have a credit card, remember?" I smile and nod at Sheila. Again, I get a little hard as I think about her naked and in bed with me. She is truly an attractive young woman.

Darla nods her head. "Let's do it, then."

"Alright." Sheila gets up from her seat and we do the same. She leads us to a chair where Darla sits down. "What would you like to get?"

I shake my head. "I'll get one a little later after I get over the sticker shock of this one. For now, I want to make this all about my wife." Sitting down nearby, I watch as Sheila begins to explain the entire process, including how ink will be pushed into the skin. Some of her remarks are very plain and a little gruesome as speaks. Though I had a basic understanding before we came here of how tattoos are made, I didn't realize just how involved they can be.

"Any questions?" Sheila asks as she looks down at Darla.

"I guess not." My wife pulls off her tee shirt and then unfastens her bra in the back while Sheila puts the chair back until it is flat and more like a padded table. Darla lays down and holds her bra in place as Sheila gloves up and reaches for a sterile gauze pad and some disinfectant.

"How long have you been doing this?" I ask as I watch her prepare my wife's bare back.

"Four years," she replies. "Right here the whole time." She doesn't look at me as she studies the drawing and my wife's back. "Hold on. Let me get a stencil." Sheila stands to her feet and goes to a large machine nearby. She turns it on and it whirs as it begins to produce a sheet of adhesive-lined paper.

"Don't talk to her and cause her to mess up," Darla pleads with me quietly. "A mistake here isn't exactly something that she will be able to erase, Leo."

"I'm guessing that's why they have a machine that makes a stencil," I say to her with a smile. I watch as Sheila checks the sheet of paper that now has a shape that is very similar to the outline of the art that my wife has selected.

"Here we are. Just to get the edges down." Sheila lines the stencil up and reaches for a small Sharpie marker. "I'm just going to make some marks to guide me, alright?" Darla nods her head and the tattoo artist begins to mark some of the borders of the design.

"So, what sort of tattoo would a guy get that says that he's a sexual and fertile guy?" I ask her.

Sheila, without cracking so much as a smile, replies, "A giant dick or a muscle car. One or the other." I get the feeling that she might not like that I'm talking to her as she works, so I sit back and get quiet as she finishes making a few marks on my wife's back.

"Will it hurt?" Darla asks her as Sheila lifts the stencil from her back.

"Life hurts," the other woman replies. "We all have to go through pain to get to something more rewarding, right? Just think about this as being one of those times in your life. It will be worth it, though." Sheila adjusts the tattoo gun as she looks over at me. "The ink won't be completely black while I'm putting it in. It darkens as it sets in."

"Okay." I'm confused as to why she tells me this.

Sensing my confusion, Sheila adds, "I don't need you telling your wife what's going on or if something doesn't look right to you. Okay?"

"So, keep my mouth shut," I chuckle.

"There you go." Sheila offers me a slight smile this time, but only briefly enough to make certain that I have understood her correctly. I sit back in my chair and watch as she begins to tattoo Darla's back.

"Shit, that stings," my wife tells her.

"It'll hurt worse tomorrow," the young woman promises as she works around the outlines of the image that is going onto her back. "We'll talk about pain management and keeping it clean when I'm finished."

"Pain management?" Darla's eyes connect with mine as she turns her head to look at me. I can see that this worries her a little. It is of some concern to me as well. Regardless, this is what we have decided to do. There's no way to turn back. The first of the ink has been laid and there is a lot more to be put into her skin before Sheila is finished with her. The fifteen hundred dollars this will cost is worth it if the tattoo comes out as sexy as it looks to be in the book of art. I smile to myself as I imagine us out on a date together, her bare back exposed to the world. Of course, in my imagination, Sheila is there too. Who says I don't have one hell of an active imagination?

Chapter Four: The Big Reveal

22

"Let's go out this evening," Darla says, which surprises me a little.

"It's Friday," I remind her as I shake my head. "Don't you have a friend who wants to go out with you?"

Darla giggles. "No, sweetie. I want to go out with you. There's a new restaurant near the school and I want to see if it's as good as some of the other teachers have been claiming." My wife smiles at me and I feel goosebumps rise along my neck and back. It's been a while since she has been so eager to spend time with me like this.

We go to the bedroom to get ready and Darla looks at her tattoo in the mirror. "I took the bandages off yesterday. It's completely healed up now. What do you think?"

My eyes move along her soft, sexy back, taking in all of the curves and strokes of the incredible artwork that runs from the base of her neck to her tailbone. Sheila did an incredible job on the tattoo and I feel more than pleased at the expenditure of so much money to get it. Darla seems to be a little more adventurous now as she reaches for a new dress that she recently bought.

"It's backless," she says after she slips it on. "Wow. She was right about how it would look, babe. I love it." I walk up to my wife and run my fingers along her bare back. Darla smiles and blushes a little as she turns to fix her hair.

"I want to show it off, Leo. I mean, it wasn't cheap and it's so beautiful." She turns and looks at me. "Don't just stand there. Put on a nice suit coat and slacks, Leo. This is a nice place, not some burger joint." I nod my head and smile before turning to find clothes to wear tonight. I can't remember the last time we have gone out together to a fancier restaurant like this. If I play my cards right, I might even get lucky tonight and get to see the long tattoo moving around just in front of me.

It takes us about an hour to get ready, but only about a quarter of that time to find the restaurant. We walk in and get a table, thanks to Darla having already called that morning to make a reservation for us. As we sit down, a server comes to our table with menus and wine glasses.

"We have an excellent Chardonnay wine for tonight if that sounds agreeable," the young woman says as she looks at the two of us.

"What do you think?" Darla smiles as she watches me nod my head. "Sure, we'll have that," she tells the young server.

"Chardonnay. Let's keep it under three glasses each, though, okay?"

"I'm not an alcoholic," my wife informs me. "Yes, I sometimes like to drink a bit too much, but it's because they're my friends. What else am I supposed to do with them?"

"I don't know. Maybe go bowling or something," I joke, causing us both to laugh.

"Miss." A different server comes up to us while the other one is gone. "Compliments of the gentleman at the table across the way." He nods his head toward a table behind Darla and across the room. The man seated there lifts his hand as if to say hello. The server then turns and leaves.

Confused, Darla looks at the glass of dark red wine that has been placed in front of her. "Um, what is this for?"

"That's not our server," I say as I look around. "And that guy over there seems to be really enthusiastic about waving to you." I look over at him, jealousy beginning to rise inside me. Why would another man send a guy's wife a glass of wine? It's a little weird.

My wife takes a sip of the wine. "Wow. This isn't the cheap stuff, Leo." She then takes another sip and shakes her head. "What did I do to get his attention?"

"I don't know." I continue to look over at the man. Should I go over to him and confront him for targeting my wife with a drink? Maybe he knows her?

"Does he look familiar to you at all?" I ask.

Darla turns and looks at him again. "Not really. I've known a lot of people, though, so I suppose it's possible that we might have met at one of the regional teacher trainings. I don't know."

I grimace. "This is odd." I look around and find another man sitting and staring at my wife's back. "The tattoo got someone's attention." I nod my head in his direction. Darla turns to look at the second man. "This is creepy," she tells me as she turns back to face me. "Way too creepy."

"Yeah, I don't know what the hell is going on."

Our server suddenly returns with the bottle of Chardonnay. "Oh. Would you prefer this wine?" She nods at the glass in Darla's hand.

"No," my wife answers. "There's a guy who sent this to me. Another server brought it over."

The young woman looks in the direction of the man. "Ah. Okay. Do you still want the Chardonnay?"

"Yes, please," I answer as I nod my head. I don't plan to let another man ruin an evening with my wife just because he's hard for her from a distance. I watch as the server pours me a glass and I take a taste of it. "This is good." I watch as she then fills my glass.

Turning to Darla, she asks, "Would you like a glass as well?"

My wife nods. "Sure. Just a half-glass, though. My husband wants me to keep a clear head." She offers me a smile as the server does as she asks.

"Would you like the bottle?"

"No, thank you," I answer the server. "We're good."

"Are you ready to order, then?"

"No. Give us a few more minutes," I reply. The young server nods her head and walks away as I consider what is going on with the two men who are staring at my wife.

"Just try to ignore them," Darla tells me before she takes a sip of the wine she received from the first stranger.

"It's difficult to ignore two sets of eyes staring at my wife," I tell her. "They both act as if you're fair game. It's like I'm not even sitting here with you."

"Is that what this is all about?" Darla giggles. "Are you getting jealous, Leo?" I can't help but smile a little as I look back over at her. Yes, I'm jealous. Just a little. However, I also feel a little turned on by the attention she is getting by the other two men. Why is this happening, though? We've been out hundreds of times as a married couple and

I don't recall ever having this experience with her in public. Why the attention now?

"It's your backless dress," I suddenly say. "That's gotten both men's attention. That's got to be why he sent the glass of wine over to you."

Darla smiles while blushing. "It's like they've never seen a woman's back." She giggles while reaching for the glass of wine that was sent to her by one of the men. I get the sense that my wife is thoroughly enjoying the attention she is getting. It's not that I can blame her, though. Some women enjoy knowing that what they're wearing has a desired effect on a man. Any man. No, what gets to me is that Darla's eyes keep darting toward the man who bought her the drink. He's handsome, probably not much older than us, and apparently has a good taste in women.

"They just haven't seen *your* back before tonight," I tell her as I reach for her hand and take it into mine. "You're sexy, babe. Everyone can see how hot you are in your new dress with that tattoo. Enjoy the attention." I don't really mean what I say, but I want to make the most of what's happening tonight. Though I'm jealous of the attention she's getting, I can't wait to see Darla's tattoo moving up and down as she rides me cowgirl style tonight.

"Pardon me?" The young server has returned to our table. "Are you ready to order?"

I look at Darla. "Would you like to order for us both?" My wife gets a little excited when she is asked to select what I eat at a restaurant. She knows that I can be a picky eater, and this allows her to force me to expand my palate just a bit more.

"Sure." She looks at the menu. "We'll each have the orange duck with a side of brazened green beans and boiled potatoes."

"A good choice." The server jots down our order onto a small notepad and then asks," can I get you anything else?"

"Yeah, you can," I say as I get a crazy idea. "Do you serve beer here?"

The server smiles. "We have both pale and dark craft beer that is of our own branding."

"Great. Send a dark one to the same guy who sent my wife this glass of wine. Tell him that her husband just wanted to return the gesture."

"Leo!" Darla's face stretches into a horrified expression as she looks over the table at me. "Don't do that."

"Oh, come on. He'll like it," I laugh.

"Yes, sir." The server smiles sheepishly before turning and leaving our table.

"This is so embarrassing," Darla says while covering her eyes with one hand for a moment. Uncovering them, she then whispers to me, "He's going to think that I'm a bitch, Leo."

"Why would he think that? And why would you even care what he thinks? The guy is hitting on my wife with a glass of wine." Grinning wickedly, I add, "Maybe I should get his phone number so that I can text him a picture of my boobs, too. Do you think he'd jerk off to seeing my chest?"

"Leo." My wife knows that I'm kidding about the chest shot, but she still worries about the drink that I've ordered for him. The message from me should be clear; she's taken. Darla is my wife and not his to take. Dammit, why can't I shake this jealousy thing?

"There she goes," I say of the server as I see her carry the glass of craft beer to the man at the other table. He says something to her at first and then his face turns a little pale. "And he gets the message." I wave at him and laugh.

"Dammit, Leo." Darla shakes her head as she looks at me. "Really? Was that necessary?"

To my surprise, the man suddenly smiles and then waves back at me. "What the *fuck?*"

"What is it?" She's too worried to turn and look at him. "What is he doing? Is he angry?"

I sigh. "No, I wouldn't call his response *anger.*"

Darla turns to look at him for a moment and then turns back to face me. "He seems pretty happy."

"Yeah. Fuck. What the hell is it with this guy? He's even drinking the damned beer." I'm confused. Giving him the beer and then waving at him should have given him the understanding, through a level of sarcasm, that I wasn't interested in him openly flirting with Darla. Instead, it almost seems to have solidified whatever fantasy he has going on inside his head.

"Please just ignore him," my wife begs me. "Don't let this go any further, Leo. You've made your point, alright? Maybe he's just not right in the head."

"Yeah, maybe," I agree while looking at my beautiful wife. "Maybe I should go knock his head off his shoulders?"

"If you do, I'm leaving this restaurant and you're sleeping on the couch for the rest of the year."

"It's March," I remind her.

"Exactly." My wife's eyes focus hard on me and I get the point. She's not going to put up with me doing anything else to try to thwart whatever this other man has going on in his head. However, this is all very odd. Plenty of women wear dresses and shirts with open backs. Surely he's seen them before. What is it about Darla that has given this guy a hardon at a culinary establishment?

"Your duck, sir." The server smiles at me as she and a young man with her place a plate in front of each of us. "How does it look?" she asks.

"Very nice," Darla answers. "Thank you."

"Please feel free to let me know if you need anything else." She smiles and turns to leave the table.

"Duck," I say with a grunt. "Dark bird meat is disgusting."

My wife smiles. "You told me to order for you, so I did. Now eat." I love my beautiful wife. She's right. I have told her that anytime I have her order or me, I will dutifully try what is on my plate. However, there's one other thing that I just can't shake from my mind as I cut into the meat and take a small bite. Why is she getting this attention from other men and why is this one man in particular so eager to piss me off? I'll probably

not be able to figure this out at the moment as I chew the piece of duck in my mouth. Sure, it's good. But I still don't like the idea of eating dark bird meat. I never have and I doubt that I ever will.

Chapter Five: Interesting Choice

"Good morning, Mrs. Glenn," I say over the phone to one of our clients. "This is Leo at Crown & Gifford Investments. How are you today?"

"I'm fine," the eighty-year-old retiree replies. "You haven't called to give me bad news, have you?"

I chuckle. "No, ma'am. As a matter of fact, your portfolio has grown by three percent since the last time we spoke. I thought we might talk about some other options for the annuity that's due to mature in a few months."

"Annuity?"

"Yes, ma'am. The one your husband opened almost twenty years ago. It's going to mature soon and I thought I would ask if you would like to put it into your regular portfolio to continue to grow your earnings."

"I have an annuity?" The older woman on the phone seems confused and I struggle to understand how to explain this better.

"Mrs. Glenn, your husband opened it and then transferred it to our accounts when he opened a portfolio here."

"My husband is dead," she says flatly.

"Uh, yes, ma'am. I know. I'm sorry." Mr. Glenn, her husband of more than fifty years, passed away three years ago. I've spoken to her many times since that time and never had so much trouble getting through to her.

"I don't want whatever you're selling. Don't call back." She suddenly hangs up the phone and I look up to see Justin staring at me from the other side of my desk.

"Mrs. Glenn, eh?"

"Yeah."

"She's got dementia. Her son's number is on the file now." I turn to my computer screen and scan to the bottom.

"Fuck," I say quietly. "I didn't know that."

"I tried to call her two weeks ago and figured it out then. She doesn't remember a lot, depending upon the time of day that you reach her. That's what her son told me when he got on the phone. He's handling everything now." Justin taps the computer screen. "His phone number is right here."

"Then why the fuck isn't his number in the primary contact line?" I shoot a look up at my friend and colleague, causing him to draw back away from my desk a little.

"Whoa, buddy. What's eating at you this morning?" I can see the concerned look on Justin's face. He really is a good friend and I shouldn't treat him so terribly.

"I'm sorry. It's just that I've had a few things on my mind lately."

"Things on your mind?" Justin reaches for a chair nearby and pulls it up to my desk. "Anything that you want to share with me?" He smiles, which causes me to smile slightly as well.

"Darla and I went to dinner on Friday evening and let's just say things got a little weird."

"Weird?" Justin raises an eyebrow.

Nodding my head, I confirm, "Weird." I pause and take a breath before explaining, "There are some things that a guy just shouldn't do, you know?"

"Like pee with the seat down? Spit on the sidewalk in front of a lady?" Justin muses.

"No, not really anything like that," I say with a laugh. "There were a couple of guys who took notice of my wife while we were out having dinner together."

Justin grins. "Okay. That's happened to me before when I was out with my ex-wife. Some guys just want what you have. It happens, buddy. You'll survive." He pats me on the shoulder like I'm a child as he smiles down at me.

"It was different," I say as I push his hand away.

"Different in what way?"

I sigh. "One of them actually sent her a glass of wine. Right to our table. While I was sitting there with her."

Justin's eyes widen. "Wow. That guy was really going for it, huh?"

"He fucking stared at her during the entire time we were there. It was really fucking creepy. I even had our server send him a beer and he had the balls to wave at me for it! What the hell is wrong with some guys?"

"Did you deck him?" my colleague asks. "I would have decked him."

"No. Darla threatened to put me on the couch for the rest of the year if I did anything else. I don't get what the fuck is wrong with some people."

"Yeah." Justin thinks for a moment. "What was she wearing? Anything a little more sexy than usual?"

I nod my head. "Yeah, a backless dress. Here, look." I have a picture of Darla wearing her dress from the back. She insisted that I take it so that she could see what it looked like from behind as her tattoo stands out. As Justin looks over the image on my phone, he raises an eyebrow.

"I've seen this before," he remarks.

"The dress is pretty common, I think. It wasn't exactly a designer label."

"No, man. That tattoo." He points to the long design stretching from the base of Darla's neck to her tailbone. "I can't quite put my finger on it, but I know that I've seen it." Justin stares hard at the image. "Can you send it to my phone?"

"Hey, just wait a minute, man..."

"No, Leo. I'm not being that way. I just want to do something." I take back my phone after giving Justin a strained look. After texting the image to him, I watch as he pulls it up and performs an image search on Google.

"It's just a tattoo," I tell him. "They had it at a tattoo studio on the other side of town. Apparently it's not all that popular, but it was really expensive."

"Holy shit." Justin begins to laugh. "Oh, man, your wife fucked up." He hands his cell phone over to me. I look at the image and what is written about it.

"Dammit. *DAMMIT!*" I shove the phone back at my colleague and get up from my chair. "What the hell am I going to do? It's too fucking huge to remove it."

"*That's what she said!*" Justin doubles over in laughter after making a reference to a television show.

"Dammit, Justin. This is serious!" I grit my teeth as I watch him sit up and heave for breath.

"What the hell is this?" Mike asks as he walks up to us. The investment firm manager seems peeved that we've disturbed the quiet atmosphere of the office.

"Look." Justin hands his phone to Mike.

"What's this?"

"It's on his wife's *back!*" Justin begins to laugh again as Mike looks from the phone to me. He actually cracks a smile.

"Was this done on purpose?" he asks as he tries to keep a straight face.

"No," I say as I try to contain my aggravation. "She didn't know that it meant that when she picked it out. The tattoo artist said it meant something like fertility."

"Oh, hell." He snorts a little as he tries to hold back a laugh. "Excuse me. I have a telephone call coming through that I need to take." Mike turns and walks quickly back to his office and closes the door behind him.

"You made him *smile!*" Justin continues to laugh hard as I look down at him. "You and your wife are royally screwed, man. *Royally screwed.* That is, if she's *down with it.*"

"Fuck you!" I almost smile as I watch as he sits back in my chair, his face red and tears beginning to stream down his face. There has not been a time before when I've seen him more humored by something since I've known him.

Justin begins to try to contain himself. "I'm sorry, Leo. It's just that this is a big problem."

"I know." I shake my head. "Darla thought it was just cool looking. So did I. Now she's wearing something that says, *'Hey, I'm in an open marriage. Come have sex with me.'*"

"You should have searched for the image before she had it put on, Leo. It's always a good idea to know what something means."

"We thought it was just a design that they came up with and that it had limited meaning to it. The lady at the tattoo studio showed it to us as if it was their original artwork." I grimace as I shake my head. "Maybe I should sue them for this."

"It wouldn't go very far," Justin replies as he wipes his eyes with his hand. "They would claim that it was just a work of art that your wife agreed to have put on her back." He takes a breath and adds, "At least it's not on her forearm or lower leg. This should be pretty easy to hide."

"She won't be able to wear a bikini. Or any other swimsuit, for that matter. Dammit, I don't know what to say to Darla. This is going to freak her out."

"Maybe it will, or maybe it won't. You won't know until you tell her what it means, Leo. Then she can figure out if she wants to hide it. I mean, there aren't exactly that many people who will know what the tattoo really means."

"There were two guys at the restaurant who obviously knew what it meant," I reply. "Out of maybe forty or so men in there. That's not a terribly low percentage, and some of the guys there might not have gotten a clear look at her back."

"Dude, that was in a finer restaurant. If you go to a place like McDonald's or Pizza Hut, I doubt anyone would know what the tattoo stands for."

"It still means that she's open for sex with other men," I complain. "Even though she's married to me. That doesn't sit well with me at all."

"Get over it, Leo. It'll be a little inside joke with your wife. Trust me. In years to come, you'll look back at this and have a good laugh with her." Justin smiles as he tries to keep from laughing again.

I get the humor in all this, I really do. If it had been Justin's girlfriend instead of my wife, I might have laughed the same way he did. Even so, it's become far too real for me. At some point, I'm going to have to tell Darla the truth about her so-called work of art that stretches the length of her back. It won't be easy to do. We paid a lot of money for her to put that tattoo on her back, and instead of having something that would be appreciated as aesthetically pleasing, we have men wanting to get into her panties.

"It's damned stupid," I say as I shake my head. "They should pay for what they've done to her. What they've done to *us*."

"You won't get anywhere by suing the tattoo parlor, Leo. Take it from me. Just move on and let this be a big lesson for the both of you." He smiles as he holds back another laugh before turning and leaving my desk.

"Fucking tattoo shop. Lying bitch." I think of the woman who put the design on Darla's back and I get a little hard again. She seemed like the sort who could be wild in bed with a guy. Surely she knew the real meaning of the tattoo before she put it on Darla's back? How could she not? If one of Darla's coworkers at the elementary school where she works sees the tattoo and knows what it means, it could cause an incredible amount of embarrassment. This is the very reason why I have to tell my wife soon about the true meaning behind the tattoo.

I sit down at my desk and collect my thoughts for a moment before getting back to work. There's nothing that can be done now except to get my work here done. With other clients to call, I am determined to be more careful than I was with Mrs. Glenn. I don't want to upset anyone with dementia, and we have plenty of elderly clients to deal with. It's best to keep my mind on this instead of thinking any further about Darla's back.

Chapter Six: No Reasonable Person

I sit on the couch beside Darla as we watch a movie on television. We've been quiet while snuggling, and that quiet seems to be getting to my wife. She looks over at me.

"Is there something bothering you?" she asks as her green eyes look at me.

I swallow hard as I consider how to phrase what I need to tell her. After pausing the movie, I reply, "Justin and I were talking about your tattoo earlier today. As well as the guys at the restaurant last Friday evening."

"Oh? And?" She waits patiently for me to give her the full story. I'm stalling, of course. How do I tell her that she has gotten a large tattoo that advertises her as being in an open marriage?

Pulling out my cell phone, I find the picture of her in the dress, Darla's back toward me. She looks at it and says, "I've seen this."

"Yeah, I know. But, what you don't understand is that Justin has seen this before as well. He did an image search and found something crazy." I swipe past the image to a screenshot of the image search. My wife's face turns pale as she looks at the information there. "I think the guys who saw it the other night were aware of what it actually means. As a matter of fact, the man who got the beer from me probably took that as some kind of appreciation for him noticing your tattoo."

Darla turns her eyes toward me. "I have a tattoo on my back that's a huge advertisement for *sex?*"

"I'm sorry, babe. I had no idea what it meant before the tattoo artist put it on you." I turn to face her better and offer, "I've looked into laser removal. It's been done before, and there's a great dermatologist in the city who can do it for around six thousand dollars. She says it will likely take around ten visits to get it all out and that there will probably be very little scarring at all."

Darla's eyes grow wide. *"Laser removal?"* She shakes her head. "That's painful, Leo. And it would be along my backbone all the way from my neck to my tailbone. I just can't do it."

"The doctor told me that they can give you some local anesthesia. You shouldn't feel anything while she's removing the tattoo."

"Just afterwards, right?" she retorts. "Dammit, Leo. How the hell could this happen to me? It's such a pretty design."

"And the tattoo artist claimed that it would look great on you. We should think about suing her." I purse my lips as I look at the concerned expression on my wife's face. "I really am sorry, babe. I'll do whatever I can to get this fixed for you."

Darla sits for a moment, quiet and thinking. "That man who sent me the wine thought I liked to have sex with other men even though I'm married?" I nod my head. "That's why he sent it to me. It's why he didn't know how upset you were when you sent him that beer. The tattoo is a huge sign that tells other men that I'm in an open marriage and looking."

"And that's why we can't let this thing stay on your back, Darla. We have the money in savings. I think you should go ahead and get started with the procedure right away."

"But, I have school," she replies as she shakes her head. "You don't understand, Leo. I can't just take time off. *Ten visits?* And what will it be like to heal? I'm sure I'll be wearing bandages on my back all the time. Someone will likely notice and begin to ask questions."

I shake my head. "Those questions will be tame in comparison to what questions you might get if someone sees the tattoo and realizes what it is."

"It can't be that common, though. I've never seen it on anyone else, Leo."

"I know. Still, it's common enough that some men will know what it means."

"And women."

I nod my head. "Yeah, and women." Sitting forward in my seat, I tell Darla, "I love you and I don't want you to have to go through this, but there's no other way other than just covering it up all the time. I know you, babe. I know you would miss your bikini in the summer. You need to get this thing taken off your back."

Darla shakes her head. "It's so pretty, though. No matter what it means, I chose it because I liked the way it would look on my back. And I'm not disappointed by it, Leo."

"Really? You're not disappointed by it? Babe, the thing marks you as being a wife in an open marriage. If other men see it and know what it means, it will attract them to you like flies on shit." I can't believe that my wife would consider not having the tattoo removed. Sure, laser removal can be time consuming and a little painful, but it's over several treatments, not all at once. It could be gone by summer and Darla would then be able to wear her bikini to the beach.

"I don't want to take it off," she confirms. "We paid for it and I like it. There's no reason to let some meaning behind it dictate whether I keep the tattoo." Darla gets up from the couch and goes to the kitchen. I stand up as well and follow her.

My wife reaches into the refrigerator for a wine cooler. After opening it, she takes a sip. "Please think about this," I tell her. "This will haunt you for the rest of your life, Darla. Let's get it taken off."

She frowns at me. "It's easy for you to demand this of me because you don't have to go through the laser removal, Leo. What if you had some other woman's name tattooed on your dick? Would you want that removed with a laser?"

"Your tattoo is on your back. Not on your pussy. It's not even a fair comparison."

"It will still *hurt.*" She stresses after putting her bottle down on the countertop. "It's along my spine. I've heard that laser removal hurts more than the original tattoo inking, and that hurt like hell. I'm not going to have it removed. End of story." Darla reaches for her drink and walks back to the living room. I've heard her use the *end of story* comment before. It means that she doesn't intend to talk about it anymore. However, I'm not finished as she sits down on the couch.

"Do you *like* showing it off?" I ask her. "Did you enjoy the fact that other men were ogling you while we ate our meal? That some jackass bought you a glass of wine?"

Her green eyes turn toward me as she brushes some of her blonde hair over her ear. "Maybe I do. Maybe I like it when others appreciate me or how I look. Is there anything really wrong with that?" Darla is defiant as she glares at me. I can see that she's set on keeping this thing, but it doesn't sit well with me.

"Other men already lust for you, babe. They want you. I see that every day. But now, with this tattoo, I have to worry that some of them might do more than just look. Some of them might try to get into your panties and fuck you. Is that what you want? Darla, do you want to screw other men?"

She looks away for a moment, obviously upset with my questions. "Not once have I given in to any man who has wanted me since we got married, Leo. Not one time. You know that I'm faithful to you, but even after several years of marriage you don't seem to appreciate that. Sure, I like to know men look at me. Most women do. But I've never cheated on you. If you think that I have, then you can fuck yourself and get out." Darla crosses her arms over her chest as she continues to glare at me.

After sighing, I reply, "I'm sorry. I don't mean to make it sound like any of this is your fault. We need to get this thing taken care of sooner rather than later, my love. If people find out about this, it could cause you problems at your school. Then it could mean that we end up with unwanted men coming to our door."

"That won't happen," she immediately answers. "No one is going to know where we live just by looking at my back, Leo. We'll be okay."

"Of course they won't, but there will be men who are around you who might be tempted to ask for your phone number or to try to give you theirs. That could get to be really embarrassing for you."

"And for you." Darla again levels her green eyes at me. "The person having the most trouble with this is you, Leo." She pauses before saying,

"I'll tell you what I'm willing to do. Go to that same tattoo shop and get this same tattoo on your back. Have it stretch all the way from your neck to your tailbone. Then, after it's finally healed, go have it removed with a laser."

I shake my head. "But, that's stupid. It would mean another fifteen-hundred dollars for the tattoo and then another six thousand dollars to remove it. Plus the time and all the other factors."

"The pain," she interjects. "You would get the pleasure of that as well."

"There's no point," I say as I get more frustrated with my wife. "Unless your point is that I should go through the same pain."

"It is!" She stands up and walks over to me. Poking her finger into my chest, my wife tells me, "I have chosen this tattoo and I like it. I don't care if there are other men who will see it and make silly assumptions about who I am and what I'm willing to do. I'll ignore every one of them as it happens. I refuse to go through the pain of laser removal just to make you feel more comfortable around other men." Darla shakes her head as she turns and walks toward our bedroom.

"So, that's it, then? You just decide on your own that you won't get the tattoo taken off? You're ignoring what I want?"

My wife turns around before going into the bedroom. "It's *my* body, Leo. Get over it or get out. It's that simple." She then closes the door and locks it. I feel a lump rise up inside my throat.

"Well, that didn't fucking go as planned," I grumble to myself as I consider whether I'll have to sleep in the living room tonight. "I don't get it. I just don't. It's a simple thing to do, and she won't do it." I turn and sit back down on the couch before continuing the movie. I doubt I'll see Darla again tonight. However, this is not over. She simply cannot keep that thing on her back for other men to see.

Chapter Seven: More Than Avocados

43

Though Darla and I had a disagreeable conversation about her tattoo the other night, we now find ourselves going to the grocery store to shop for some groceries on a Saturday morning. The air is crisp and chilly, so my wife wears a light jacket while I have decided to wear a long sleeve shirt. After we walk into the store, we get a cart and Darla almost immediately stops to pull off her jacket.

"It's warmer inside," she says while pulling it off. She places the jacket onto the side of the grocery cart. It takes me a moment to notice her shirt, but I do finally notice it with a gasp.

"What the hell is *this?*" I whisper as I look at the plunging back of the shirt. "That tattoo is visible, babe. Cover it up." I can't believe that Darla has intentionally worn this shirt. She knows what the tattoo means and how men will react if they understand it.

"It's just a tattoo," she replies as we walk through the store. "Don't draw attention to it and we'll be just fine."

"Don't draw attention to it?" I respond sardonically. "If you had a neon sign hanging around your neck it wouldn't be any more conspicuous than your back." I grimace as I look around the store. "There are people here who might know what it means, Darla. And the way you're showing it off is going to tell those people that you intend to find someone who's interested in the message of the tattoo."

"It's not my problem if the tattoo means something else," she answers while stopping to look at some avocados. "You know, it's been a while since we have had guacamole. Should I get a few of these and make us some?"

"Dammit, Darla," I fume as I try to keep from raising my voice to a level that will get other people's attention. "Put your jacket on. Please. Don't do this to us."

She turns while holding a couple of avocados. "Don't do this to *us,* or to *you?*"

"You know what I mean."

"Yeah, I do. It's not bothering me, sweetheart. It really shouldn't be bothering you, either. No one has come up to me or stared at me so far."

"Because I'm trying to keep your back hidden," I say while looking around. "Someone will eventually see it and they will know what it is. Or they will Google the image and find out what it means. Please, babe. Put the jacket back on." I watch as Darla gets a clear bag from a roll nearby. She drops two avocados into the bag and ties it closed before putting it into the grocery cart.

"It's too warm in here to wear my jacket," she tells me calmly. "Let's look at the oranges and tangerines. Which would you prefer, Leo?"

I clench my jaw as I watch Darla move to the citrus fruits and look them over. I'm convinced that she's doing this on purpose just to get to me. There's no other reason to have worn the shirt she has on and she already knew that it would peeve me. Why would she want to cause me this angst today? We're shopping for groceries, not fishing for lustful men. Where the fuck did she get a tee shirt that has a plunging back to show off her tattoo, anyway?

"Don't pout," my wife says as she returns with a bag of tangerines. "You know that I hate it when you do that."

"I'm not pouting," I protest. We continue walking around the store until we get to the bread aisle. I suddenly notice a young man walking up to us. At first, I think that he might be an employee because he's dressed in a red tee shirt and blue jeans, just as many of the employees happen to be.

"Hey," he says with an impish grin as he looks at us. "I'm Kyle."

"Hello, Kyle," Darla replies with a smile.

"Yeah, hello," I add warily.

"Um, so, I wanted to give you this." He hands my wife a business card. "I work at that dealership as an assistant sales manager. My personal number is on the bottom of the card." He points toward the phone number. "Are you two from around here?"

"We live in the city, yes," I reply. "Car dealership?"

"One of the biggest in the state," he answers. "We have all sorts of models, both foreign and domestic." Kyle smiles again, a dimple appearing on one cheek. Darla is a sucker for dimples and she blushes a little as she returns a smile.

"We have a car," I tell him. "A good one. Maybe in a couple of years we'll be looking for one."

"Sure. That would be great." The young assistant sales manager doesn't seem so interested in selling us a car as he continues to look at my wife.

"Did you grow up here?" Darla asks.

"I sure did."

"And how old are you?" It's a question that I was about to ask him, but my wife has beaten me to it.

"Twenty-three," he answers.

"And an assistant sales manager already?" I raise an eyebrow as I look at him.

Kyle nods his head. "I started with the dealership when I was fifteen by washing and detailing used cars for my uncle."

"Ah, okay. That answers it," I chuckle. "Your uncle owns it and so you're the assistant sales manager." Though I don't mean to point out the obvious so harshly, I do. After all, he seems to be almost flirting with Darla.

"Yeah, I know. He gave me the job. But I am good at it. Sales are up and I have a degree in Business Administration from the university. I work hard." He turns his attention to my wife. "So, you're really looking?"

"Looking?" Darla says questioningly.

Kyle nods at her shirt. "Your back says you're open. Are you?"

"For fuck's sake." I step back while shaking my head. "The tattoo. *Again.*"

"I'm sorry?" Kyle seems confused.

Darla puts a hand on his forearm. "You know what the tattoo means?"

"Yeah, I do. Don't you?"

"We know," she confirms. "It's just that, this isn't the way my husband expected things to go when I got it."

"Oh." He turns his blue eyes to look at me. "Man, I'm sorry. I didn't mean to be so forward. It's just that I've never seen anyone with that tattoo before, so I figured I would just go for it." Kyle laughs a little before adding, "It's a good thing, though. If we had hooked up, my girlfriend might have found out and then I would have been in a lot of trouble."

"Thank you for noticing, though," Darla says to him. Kyle nods his head and turns to walk back down the aisle and then around the corner.

"Thank you for noticing?" I quietly say to her. "Why would you say that to him?"

She shrugs her shoulders. "I don't know. I guess it's nice to know that a young man would see the tattoo and instantly think that I'm worth the effort to get to know."

"Darla, this isn't funny," I tell her as I see a slight grin on her face. "He's a stranger. He wanted to have sex with you."

"He's not so much of a stranger, Leo. He introduced himself. He's Kyle." She giggles a little.

"Dammit. You can't lead guys on like that. What if he had been someone who's serious about that sort of thing? Maybe a guy who's a little older and experienced in this lifestyle? You might piss the guy off when you deny him and then get us both hurt or killed."

"I don't think that would happen," she retorts.

Getting closer to my wife, I tell her, "I saw a video of a buck that went after a hunter after he sprayed doe urine onto his pants leg. *Doe urine.* The buck thought he was going to find a girlfriend when he came to him, but when he saw it wasn't a doe he charged the man and nearly killed him. Darla, stop fucking around with this nonsense. You're not in an open marriage."

She sighs and looks up at me with her green eyes. "Maybe I want to be."

"What to be what?"

"In an open marriage, Leo. Maybe I want to be available for guys like Kyle once in a while." Darla's focus stays on me as I try to understand what she really means.

"But...wait."

"Haven't you ever wondered what it would be like to have sex with someone else? Don't you want to feel another woman in your arms once in a while? Sweetie, we could do that if we really wanted to. Maybe this tattoo is just what we need."

Shaking my head, I reply, "You can't be serious, babe. There's no way that you really want to screw some other man. Kyle...that guy is ten years younger than you. He's barely out of college."

"But he's attractive, Leo. And I'll bet that he would be great in bed."

"I can't believe that we're having this conversation in the middle of the fucking grocery store." I step back and look at her. "Honestly, Darla, you're scaring me just a little bit. We're *married* to each other. At no point did we agree to have an open marriage."

"We should really reconsider it," she answers quickly. "Look, this whole thing with the tattoo and the attention that I've gotten has caused me to start thinking. You and I have been a little too timid in what we do together sexually. We need to expand our horizons and try some new things once in a while. Having sex with other people won't mean that we don't love each other anymore. It just means that we'll be having sex with other people once in a while."

"No," I say flatly. "There's no way that we can do that. Darla..."

"Excuse me," a man just a little older than me says as he interrupts. "I love the tattoo on your back."

"Well, thank you," Darla says while blushing a little.

"You know what it means, right? I'm just checking because it's not something that is very common." He smiles, his perfectly straight white teeth in stark contrast to his tan skin.

"We know what it means, and no, she's not available," I say to him as I step between the man and my wife.

"Leo, stop it."

"I don't mean anything by it," the man says as he puts up his hands in front of him and backs away. "Have a good day." He leaves the aisle and I turn to look at Darla.

"You're embarrassing me," she tells me under her breath.

"You're embarrassing *both* of us," I counter. "You need to put that damned jacket back on."

"Why? What does it matter what the hell I wear, Leo? People are always making assumptions about me. Am I thin enough? Do I have enough makeup on? Am I a good wife? All these fucking assumptions." She turns and pushes the cart in front of us.

"We're not in an open marriage."

She stops and turns around. Holding Kyle's business card in her hand, she tells me, "I'm going to call him and invite him to have dinner with us."

"You can't do that."

"Why not?" she asks while glaring at me. "It's a free country, Leo."

"Because we're married. Darla, think about what you're doing. You can't go out on a date with another man. It's not right."

She shakes her head. "I'm going to invite him to join us for dinner. It's not a real date. If you want to come along, you can feel free to do so. But you're not going to tell me what to do." I'm shocked to hear her talk to me like this. Why would Darla risk our marriage over some guy who works in a car dealership owned by his uncle? The whole thing seems counterintuitive to me, but I realize that there's not much that I can do about it right now. Not without having a huge argument with Darla in the middle of the grocery store.

"I don't like it, babe. I can't approve of it."

"And you don't have to," she responds. "Feel free to come with me if you want. You can keep an eye on us and make sure that we're not doing anything we shouldn't be doing in the middle of a restaurant in public."

Against my better judgment, I reply, "Fine. I'll go. But don't expect me to like this guy. He's looking for one thing, Darla. *One* thing."

"I know," she replies. "And we'll see whether he gets that one thing or not." She turns and begins to push the cart again, a smile on her face. I'm out of ideas as to what I can say to her to get my wife to reconsider her decision. The fact is, she hasn't had sex with him yet and this could simply be a way for her to allow someone else besides me to stroke her ego just a little bit. Darla has a lot of attention being paid to her by other men because of her new tattoo. I suppose I should let her enjoy this limelight for just a little while. But only for a little while. Then I want something done about that damned tattoo.

Chapter Eight: Meeting Up

51

I've been on edge all day long. As a matter of fact, I've felt a little nauseous since last weekend when we met Kyle in the grocery store and he came up to Darla to give her his business card with his personal phone number. Things have been quiet between my wife and I as well, which hasn't helped things between us. I worry that she might have decided to go too far with this open marriage thing.

"Relax," Darla says to me as we are seated at a table. "He'll be here soon."

I shake my head. "I don't like this. Not one bit." Looking around, I can see that the restaurant is filled almost to capacity. It's a nice Italian eatery with all sorts of things on the menu that we have enjoyed together before. Unfortunately, my memories of this place are about to be spoiled by the presence of a man who wants to have sex with the love of my life.

"Relax," she says again as a server gives us our menus. "One more," Darla says to him. "We have another coming soon."

"Yes, ma'am." He hands her a third menu and she puts it beside her on the table. "Would you like anything to drink?"

"A berry limeade," she answers with a smile on her face. The restaurant is known for its fruity drink concoctions.

"Water," I reply flatly as I hand the menu back to the young man. "I'm no very hungry tonight."

"Not hungry?" Darla looks across the table at me. "You're joking, right?"

"I'm fine," I tell her. "All I need is water."

"Right away, sir." The man smiles and nods before leaving our table.

"Stop sulking."

"So, I was pouting at the store before and now I'm *sulking*. What's the difference?" I shake my head as I look back at her.

Darla frowns. "This can either be a nice time together or you can make it more difficult, Leo. It's completely up to you. I would prefer that we all three get to know each other really well. Don't you want to make another friend?"

"Another friend?" I chuckle. "Yeah, that's what I would call the guy who wants to diddle my wife. A *friend.* An honest, true-blue friend." I turn to look around the restaurant. "Damned place is crowded. Maybe you should have worn that fucking dress or even the tee shirt with the back open, Darla. There are lots of men here who might have loved seeing your tattoo and sending you drinks."

"Stop it," she demands. "You're being childish."

"And what are you being?" I ask. "Certainly not considerate of me or my feelings. I told you that I didn't want you to press this thing. He's a fucking kid."

"He's twenty-three," Darla retorts. "He's been able to have a legal drink for two years. So, no, he's definitely not a kid." She looks up and her eyes get wide as she smiles. "And here he is!" My wife stands up from her seat and quickly hugs the young man as he walks up to our table. "I'm so glad that you're here."

"Me too," Kyle replies. I simply sit and look up at him. He knows that I'm not all that keen on what's happening here. No words are necessary to convey that message.

"Have a seat," my wife says to him. Kyle sits down next to her and smiles as he moves the menu around. "We've ordered our drinks already. Would you like anything?"

"Sure. I'll have whatever you're having."

"Real men have water," I say as I raise an eyebrow.

"Really, Leo? Can't you just let it drop?"

"I don't think that I can." The server comes to the table and delivers our two drinks.

Kyle looks up at him when he asks about his drink. "Water, please. It's what real men drink." Darla smiles as she blushes. One point to the guy who has decided to call me out with a glass of water.

"I'm sorry about Leo, Kyle. He's been in a rotten mood since I got the tattoo."

"I understand," he replies. "When you told me on the phone that it was an accident, I thought it was pretty funny. The fact that they offer it as part of their notebook in a tattoo parlor is weird."

Darla smiles at the young man. It's obvious that she's attracted to him. She wants Kyle in the same way that I want her. This scares me as I consider what to say or do next. On the one hand, I don't want to upset my wife so much. But on the other hand, this is total madness at its finest. I don't want Kyle to screw my wife.

"You really don't like me, do you?" he asks as he looks over at me.

I shake my head. "It has nothing to do with whether I like you or not. The fact of the matter is that we didn't mean to put off the vibe that you got from Darla's tattoo. It was a mistake and I've asked her to get it removed."

My wife frowns. "He wants me to have a laser treatment done. Ten visits to the doctor to get rid of it. After careful consideration, I have refused the treatment."

"You don't have cancer," I tell her. "It's a procedure, not a treatment."

"Whatever, Leo. It's still very invasive and very painful."

"*Minimally* invasive and you would have some happy pills to make things better. Honestly, it wouldn't be all that terrible." I look over at Kyle. "When you get married, keep in mind that the woman in the relationship will do as she pleases. Especially when her husband asks her not to."

"I'll try to keep that in mind," Kyle replies with a chuckle.

"Are you ready to order?" the server asks as he puts a glass of water in front of the young man.

"We are," Darla replies. "I'll have the grilled chicken caesar salad, please. Leave the dressing on the side."

"Alright. And you, sir?"

Kyle replies, "How about the parmesan stuffed chicken, please."

"With bread?" Kyle nods. "Very good. And you, sir?"

I sigh. "I told you earlier that I'm not hungry," I answer as I shake my head. "I don't want any damned food."

"Calm down," Darla whispers as she leans over the table toward me.

"I'm sorry, sir. I forgot." He offers a smile as he picks up the last two menus before leaving our table.

"Look, I think it might be a good idea if I get out of here," Kyle says as he lays a twenty-dollar-bill on the table in front of him.

"Please don't," my wife replies. "He's just being an ass."

I sigh. "Yeah, just sit down and enjoy the meal, Kyle. I'll shut up." I lean back in my seat as I look around the restaurant again. How I wish I could be at any other table besides this one at the moment.

"So, you recognized the tattoo. You haven't done this before, have you?" Darla asks him.

Kyle shakes his head. "No, I haven't. As a matter of fact I'm pretty nervous about being here with you."

My wife pats his hand softly. "You don't have anything to worry about with me. We're...*I'm* a nice person."

"And I'm not, apparently," I grumble.

"To be truthful, I have a girlfriend and we're pretty serious. I think I might propose to her soon."

"Oh, congratulations." My wife seems genuinely happy at the news. Yet, in her mind, she sees herself riding this guy. It turns me on as I think about what Kyle's girlfriend might think if she walked in on him boning Darla. I would pay to see that. Then again, maybe I could fuck the girlfriend for revenge. Oh, hell. My cock's hard again.

"I don't want her to know about this. Any of this. All I want is a different experience."

I lean forward and allow a half-smile to fill my face. "You want to have sex with my wife, right?"

Kyle swallows hard. "Yes. I would." He averts his eyes for a moment before looking back at me. "I'm sorry that it sounds so nasty, but I do. If you'll let me."

Looking back at Darla, I ask, "Is that what you want, too?"

"You know that it is," she whispers back just before she looks around the restaurant to see if anyone else is close enough to hear her. "Just keep your voice down, Leo. Okay?"

My cock is hard. I can't really explain why, but the thought of Kyle's dick buried deep inside Darla's snapper is causing me to lust for watching it happen in person. To see my wife fucked by another man, though viscerally disgusting at first, is beginning to grow on me as an idea. Could I do it? Could I sit back and let Kyle have sex with my wife while I do nothing to stop them?"

"I know I'm a stranger, but I'm a good lover in bed. I will do anything it takes to make you happy," he tells Darla. "Anything at all."

Her cheeks blush as she looks down for a moment and then back up to me. "He says he'll do anything for me that I want, Leo. I know you get a little excited when we talk about this in bed. If you'll give him a chance with me, I don't think you'll be disappointed." My wife reaches for his bicep and squeezes it with her hand. "And you're muscular, too."

"I work out some," he replies while turning red.

"Tell us about your girlfriend," I say as I sit back in my seat. "What's she like?"

Kyle licks his lips before taking a quick drink from a glass of water in front of him. "Um, well, she's tall, about five-nine, and very beautiful. She has brown hair and blue eyes and she's just finishing up her senior year at the university."

I nod my head. "Okay. What's she like in bed?"

"*Leo,*" Darla complains as she turns her green eyes toward me and glares.

"No, really. If you're going to have my wife in bed, I want to know some things about her. How's your girlfriend in bed?" My cock throbs inside my pants as I pre-come a little.

Kyle again turns red. "Well, she's good," he begins as he looks uneasily at me. He bites his lip for a moment before continuing, "She likes a lot of stuff."

"Does she like to blow you?" I ask.

"Leo, please." Darla looks around. "Someone will hear you."

I smile. "I'll try to keep it down." I turn to look at the young man as I await his response to the question.

Kyle nods his head. "She does that, yeah."

"And is she good at it? Does she deepthroat you and let you come inside her mouth?" There's a large amount of pre-come that suddenly oozes from my cock. I'm certain that I've probably wet down the front of my pants a little as my cheeks burn.

Again, he nods his head, but says, "I come in her mouth but she can't swallow it."

"She can't?" Darla turns her eyes toward him, a look of pity on her face. I'm not sure whether it's Kyle's answer or my wife's expression that causes me to become hornier, but it's one or the other. Possibly a little of both.

"She gags a little," he tells us while looking down. "I'm sorry, this is embarrassing to talk about."

"And what about sex? Does she like you to put her legs back and get deep inside her? Or maybe she likes doggystyle?"

"Here you are," the server says as he delivers the two plates of food to my wife and her prospective lover. "Can I get you anything else?"

Darla looks up at him. "No, thank you. It looks very delicious." The man bows slightly before leaving our table. "You don't have to answer that," she says to Kyle as she turns her attention back to him. "He's just trying to scare you off."

"No, I'm not," I reply. "As a matter of fact, I think I like where this is all going.

My wife seems shocked. "Really? You're okay with this?"

I nod my head. "If Kyle will answer my question."

He looks over at me tentatively. "My girlfriend won't do the doggystyle thing. She says it's too degrading, as if I'm treating her like an animal. Jenny likes to look into my eyes while we're having sex."

"That's understandable," Darla says with a smile. "But there's nothing wrong with a little sex while on all-fours." My cock throbs as I see the two of them look at each other. Yes, I want this to happen. I want to see Kyle plunge his hard cock into my wife over and over again. I want to see her come with another man. My mind swims with the possibilities as I watch them turn their attention to their food.

"After you finish eating, we'll get a hotel room."

"Really?" Darla seems just as surprised at this as she was just minutes ago at my admission that I want to watch them have sex together.

"Yeah. We should just do it."

"I'm down with that," Kyle answers with a big smile. Darla nods her head as she blushes and then takes a bite of her food. I sit back and watch them eat, my manhood continuing to dribble pre-come from my pisshole. Tonight is going to be great fun as my wife shows the young man a good time in bed. I just know it.

Chapter Nine: Hooking Up

59

We walk quietly into the hotel room, our thoughts undoubtedly on what is going to happen very soon. Darla goes to the king-size bed and sits down on the edge. Kyle does the same, but not right against her. He's acting a bit bashful, though he's the one who came up to us in the grocery store. He's the one who has asked to have sex with my wife.

I close the door and walk over to a chair where I sit down. I smile at Darla. "Babe, I'm just here to watch. You two can do whatever you want."

She smiles demurely at me before turning to face Kyle. "Are you comfortable here? Do you need anything?"

"No, I'm fine," he replies, his voice trembling a little. It makes me horny to see the way he regards Darla. Kyle wants her and he can barely stand it. However, I'm sure the thought of his girlfriend is still weighing heavily on his mind.

"Let me help you." Darla gets up from the bed and goes to where he's sitting. She bends down toward him and kisses the young man on the lips. He returns the kiss, putting his hands on her hips as they allow each other's tongues to move in and out of their mouths. Kyle is a passionate kisser, there's no denying that. He obviously likes to feel a woman's lips on his own. How fucking hot it is to see my wife biting at the lips of another man.

Darla pulls away from him and reaches down to the hem of her blouse. She pulls up on it and removes it without bothering to unbutton it. Her perky breasts move a little just behind the pale blue bra that she's wearing. The young man reaches up and works on the clasp between the two cups of the bra. Soon, Darla's breasts pop out from behind the fabric and Kyle bends forward to kiss one of her nipples. My wife's athletic body bucks a little as she pulls close to her and wraps her arms around his head.

"Oh, Kyle," she moans as he nips at her perky areola. "Fuck. You're going to drive me insane, do you know that?" Darla whimpers as she closes her eyes and simply enjoys the attention that she's getting from him. I reach down and unzip my pants so that I can pull my cock out and stroke it lightly. Pre-come is oozing from the tip of it and I use it as a lubricant as I run my fingers over it.

Darla reaches down and begins to unbutton Kyle's shirt. He helps her and soon his muscular upper body is in view. My wife's eyes grow large as she takes in the smooth chest of the young man, his muscles bulging as he grapples with her body. There's no doubt now as to the seriousness of the young man's workout regimen. I would almost call him a bodybuilder.

"I can't believe that you're really doing this with me," he says quietly as he reaches for her skirt. Kyle pushes it to the floor to reveal Darla's thong panties. She moans as he pulls these down and then runs his fingers over her smoothly waxed muff.

"Oh, *fuck*," she groans as he pushes one of his digits into her wet hole. Kyle fingers my wife for a minute or two as he bends forward and takes one of her nipples back into his mouth once again. "You're driving me fucking crazy."

Darla backs away and goes to her knees on the floor in front of the young man. She unfastens his pants and he lets her pull them off of him. His cock is large and pulsating, maybe nine inches in length as well as girthy. Kyle's girlfriend must be a proud woman to have that monster shaft inside her. I'm amazed as my wife goes down and pushes his large rod into her mouth.

"Darla," he whispers out as if he's worried that someone might hear him. His body flexes as her lips wrap tightly around his thick shaft. Kyle breathes hard as she moves up and down his cock very slowly. I know this technique very well. Darla is able to get me to come quickly by gently sucking on me while moving so slowly up and down my johnson. The sensation is almost as if someone is teasing you with their hands, only getting you to the precipice to simply make you wait a little longer for the climax. Darla often will then grab my balls and pull on them while sucking harder, causing me to spurt hard and long. My wife is a fucking beast when it comes to giving a guy head.

"Ack." She gags a little as she seats the head of his large phallus deep inside the back of her tight throat. I smile and pull hard on my own cock as I watch Darla's face turn a little red while she attempts to make the young man very happy.

"Oh, shit, *I'll pop,*" he warns her. "I don't want to come inside your mouth. Darla, please." My wife pulls up slowly as Kyle grips the covers on either side of him on the bed.

"Too much?" She looks up and smiles at him.

"I'm about to come," he tells my wife. "I want to come inside your pussy."

"You can come in both," she tells him. Then Darla goes back down on the young man. Kyle bucks a little as he looks over at me, his face turning a deep red.

"Fuck...*UHHHH!!!*" He comes hard as he spunks into Darla's waiting throat. *"Ohhhh...FUCK!!!"* Gritting his teeth, Kyle puts his hands on my wife's head as she swallows wave after wave of his thick man gravy. I can see by the look on his face that he's not experienced a blow job quite like this before. *"Shit...OHHHH!!!"* His toes point hard as he finishes shooting his wad into my wife's tight throat. She doesn't gag except for once or twice as she finishes swallowing his salty load.

Darla lifts her head up while wiping her mouth with her hand. "How was that?"

Kyle's face is still red as his body trembles from the experience. "I've never had one like that before. My girlfriend won't swallow at all."

"That's why I did it for you," my wife replies. She stands up and kisses him deeply again, her ball juice breath mixing with his as their tongues once again go in and out of each other's mouths.

The muscular man takes hold of Darla and pushes her to the bed beside him. He then rolls over and spreads her legs before putting his face between her legs. Darla's eyes widen as she feels his tongue move over her clit as he begins to eat her out.

"Kyle," she whimpers as she reaches down and puts her fingers in his light hair. The younger man feasts upon her pecan in a way that only a man his age would dare. He pushes her legs back and finds her asshole, running his tongue from there to her awaiting lady bit. Darla bucks a little as she moves her hands back to her chest to play with her nipples. I stroke my cock hard as I watch him enjoy my wife's pudding.

"Lick her little pecan," I say as I watch the two of them on the bed together. "Fuck, yeah." My wife's ass begins to grind into the bed as he continues to enjoy her sweet pussy. Darla creams a lot when I'm eating her out. Her juices are light and sweet and sometimes she squirts a little when she comes. I wonder if Kyle will make her come like that? My question is soon answered.

"Stop," Darla says to him. Kyle looks up at her.

"Am I doing something wrong?" he asks with a confused look on his face.

"No, sweetie. You're doing it really well." My wife rolls over to her stomach and then rises to her hands and knees. Her ass cheeks spread and Kyle is given an eyeful of her perfectly smooth asshole and pussy. He moves closer to her and buries his nose and mouth between her cheeks. "Dammit. Oh, fuck. *Fuck...*" Darla loves being rimmed, and Kyle seems to know exactly what he's doing here, too. Her fingers grip the bed covers hard as he puts his hands on her ass and works his tongue into her puckered back door.

I almost come, stopping only as I grip my cock tightly and then will my balls not to jettison their genetic soup. Seeing Kyle enjoy Darla's snapper as well as her asshole turns me on and I can't see myself holding out very much longer. I'm going to spurt soon, but I want to wait until my wife is orgasming.

"I want to come inside you," Kyle tells her as he pulls her to the edge of the bed and then slides his large cock into her wet hole.

"Fuck! *OH!*" Her body quakes as he finds her cervix easily, hammering it with each inward thrust. *"Ah...OW!!! FUCK!!"* His large balls slap against Darla's labia as he shoves his erect phallus deep into her womb. Kyle moves a finger along a part of her back tattoo as he holds her hip with his other hand. He doesn't get this kind of action with his girlfriend, which is why he is probably going for it with such gusto right now.

"You're so tight," he growls as he pulls hard on my wife's ass. "This feels so good. Darla, I want to come inside you. Can I come inside you?"

My wife huffs as she closes her eyes, her breasts wagging to and fro as the man behind her uses her for his own personal penis pouch. "Come inside me, Kyle! *Please!*" She moves her ass around each time he pushes into her. Darla is making sure that each stroke makes contact with her highly sensitive G-spot.

"I don't think that I can keep from nutting inside you soon," he tells her. "Oh, fuck, you feel so awesome." His muscles flex as he pulls my wife toward him hard, their bare bodies slapping against each other so loudly that I wonder if there are people in the room next door who can hear them.

"Uh...Kyle...*uhhhh...*" Darla orgasms and her toes point behind her hard as the young man continues to pound her wet pussy. *"Ahhhhhhh...ohhhhhhh..."* The bed begins to move a little along the floor as he quickens his pace. I can tell by his face that he's going to shoot his wad into my wife very soon. I also feel as if I might come as well. *"Ohhhhh...fuuuccckkk..."*

"So tight...oh...*fuck...*" Kyle pushes his cock as deep as he can into my wife and stops for a moment as he releases his first volley of little soldiers against her cervix. *"Nahhhhh!!!"* He pulls back and begins to thrust again with his second and thirt spurts. *"Gaaaaahhhh..."*

"SHIT!!!" I suddenly spurt, a long stream of white man gravy launching from the tip of my hard pecker and landing on the floor in front of me. *"Dammit. UHHHH!!!"* I stroke my cock hard and fast as I keep watching the two of them on the bed together.

"Kyle...fuck...ohhhh..." Darla holds on hard as her body begins to finish its orgasm. She's still tense as she drops her face to the bed and Kyle finishes spunking into her.

"Oh, baby. Oh, baby." He slows his thrusts and relaxes as he just enjoys the soft feeling of her hole. Slowly, his manly jism oozes from around his cock and out of my wife's tight muff hole. Kyle pulls out and lays down on the bed beside Darla.

"That was great," she says between breaths while smiling. "Kyle, you must have one happy girlfriend. You know what you're doing in bed. I can't believe she doesn't like doggystyle sex, though. That doesn't make any sense."

He waves his hands around just over where he's laying. "I don't understand it either. I just know that she thinks it's as if I'm treating her like an animal. I told her that I don't fuck other animals. Just humans." We all laugh and he reaches over to touch Darla's nude body. "You are the best I've ever had. I just want you to know that."

"You're fucking right she is," I say with a chuckle. "She's the best that anyone could have." I smile. "Of course, I am a little biased in that assessment, I suppose."

"Just a little?" Darla looks over at me, her green eyes bright and sexy. Holy shit I would fuck her right now, even with Kyle's ball juice inside her pussy, if I had anything left to offer her. My cock is limp now and the mess I've made is waiting on the floor and the edge of the seat to be cleaned up.

"You're the greatest," I tell her. "This was so damned sexy. I can't believe that I was against this at first."

"Well, I'm glad that you liked it." Darla looks over at Kyle. "I hope this doesn't turn you off of your girlfriend."

He shakes his head. "No, I really do love her. I just wanted to see what this would be like before I propose to her."

"You might have to get her to let you do doggystyle with her," I tell him. "She might not want to right now, but if you get her worked up enough she might do it for you."

"She might," he agrees. "Or, I can always just find someone who will." Kyle smiles as he looks at the two of us.

"Smart plan, buddy." We all laugh and enjoy just talking for a little while before getting dressed. Darla and I have some thinking to do concerning what's happened with the young man. Things will be different for the two of us, no matter what we might think at the moment. She's had sex with another man and I sat by and watched her do it. We need to come to understand what this means in our marriage. Thankfully, it's the weekend and we can spend plenty of time talking as much as we need to.

Chapter Ten: More Ink

67

"You know that you want me to do it again, Leo." Though I don't turn to look at Darla as she walks beside me, I get the feeling that she's smiling from ear-to-ear.

"Do it again? Why would you want to do that again, babe? You've done it once already. It's my turn to have a little fun."

"Your turn?" My wife huffs a little as we stop in front of the small coffee shop. It's not often that she wants to go for a walk early on a Saturday morning, but today is a little different for both of us. Sex has been on our minds all night long.

"Sure. That would be fair, right? You got to screw Kyle, and I figure that I might reach out to his girlfriend and see if she wants a turn on the Leo turnstile." I make a motion in front of my pants as if something is spinning around on it.

"You're disgusting," Darla giggles as she punches me in the arm.

"Oh, so it's disgusting if I want a turn with another woman? Honestly, babe, I thought we always wanted to be fair with each other." Though I might sound as if I'm just joking around with my beautiful wife, I do think that it would be nice to be able to have sex with another woman. The kink for me would be that Darla could sit back and masturbate while she watches the two of us together.

"Leo, seriously." We walk into the coffee shop as she continues to smile. Darla walks up to the counter as I stay just behind her.

"What can I get you?" the attractive young barista asks.

"I'll have the mocha caramel shot with whipped cream," Darla tells her. The barista nods her head. "And for you?"

"Well, your phone number would be a nice start," I joke.

Darla elbows me. "Hey." She shakes her head and tells the young woman, "He's really trying me this morning." The two ladies laugh.

"I guess I'll go with a java chiller, salted caramel."

"I'll get you both fixed right up." She turns and begins to work on our drinks as Darla turns to look at me.

"Leo, you're being just a little naughty." Her smile and a wink lets me know that she doesn't take seriously my attempt to get the young barista's phone number. Sure, there's little chance that I could get that phone number even if I were seriously wanting it, but I'm horny enough this morning to flirt with someone like her.

Just a couple of minutes later, the barista has our drinks ready. "On the house," she tells us as Darla attempts to hand her a debit card.

"Really?" I raise an eyebrow.

"You made my morning." The barista smiles and goes down the counter to help another customer.

"Okay. I guess your silliness got us some free drinks." Darla gives me a wry look as we walk over to a small table near a window.

"Hey, she likes me," I chuckle. "I've still got it." We both begin to drink from our cups after we settle into our seats.

My wife smiles as she thinks for a moment. "I had fun with him, Leo. A lot of fun. I think this is something that I could get used to doing once in a while."

"Really?" Though it was easy to see that she liked having sex with Kyle, I'm surprised that she's thinking about doing this as a longterm thing.

"Yeah. I know it seems weird that I would want to do something like that again, but it was just so much fun." Her green eyes focus on me. "Of course, I would want you to be there each time it happened. I think you made it even better for me, Leo. The thought of you there just made me..." She stumbles for the word.

"*Hornier*," I offer.

Her face turns a little red as she looks around. "Hornier," she repeats quietly. "That's it, I guess." Darla brushes back her blonde hair over one ear and takes another sip of her coffee. She's beautiful and I love being around her. Seeing my wife have fun with the younger man was one of the most exciting things I've ever seen. I wouldn't mind seeing her with him again.

"So, when do you want to see Kyle again?" I ask.

Darla shakes her head. "Not him. Someone else. I want each time to be with a different man." My cock stiffens as my wife tells me this.

"Really? Damn, babe. That's kinda hot." I reach down and move my growing pole around inside my pants.

"Sure. I want to sample as many of them as I can."

"Fuck." I smile wickedly.

"Oh, hey, we need to go. We have things to do today." Darla stands up. "I'll meet you outside. I need to call Becky and see if we're still on for Friday night."

"Another bender?" I joke while shaking my head.

"No. Her friend is getting married and I'm going to go shopping for some things with her. There will be absolutely zero alcohol, sweetheart. I promise." Darla smiles before turning and slipping out of the coffee shop to go to the sidewalk. I get up and look over at the counter. The young barista is standing there with an empty cup in one hand. Our eyes meet before she lifts the cup a little and points to the underside of it. It takes a moment for me to understand what she's trying to tell me. When I finally get the hint, I lift my own cup and look at the bottom of it. The name *Kari* is written there, along with a phone number and a little heart. Goosebumps suddenly rise along the back of my neck as my body shakes with sexual energy. I look back over at the young barista. She winks at me before turning to help another customer at the counter.

"*Shit,*" I say under my breath as I begin to smile. My week is only getting better as I make my way out of the coffee shop to join my wife.

We begin to walk as Darla talks on the phone with her friend. Yes. She should absolutely enjoy the company of another man. And yes, I should call Kari. Quietly, of course, and see if she's up to a spin on Leo's turnstile. If so, who knows where this could go? I can't wait to find out.

THE END

Don't miss out!

Visit the website below and you can sign up to receive emails whenever Karly Violet publishes a new book. There's no charge and no obligation.

https://books2read.com/r/B-A-GIXE-LHPRB

BOOKS 2 READ

Connecting independent readers to independent writers.

Did you love *Hotwife Tattoo - A Wife Watching Multiple Partner Hotwife Romance Novel*? Then you should read *Hotwife Sugar Book 1*[1] by Karly Violet and Scott Park!

Bored Housewife Seeking Older Rich Man For Intimacy!

Kevin stumbled across the Sugar Dating website and decided to browse to kill some timeThe website's motto was clear - Connecting Beautiful Women With Rich Men!As he scolled, Kevin had to admit the women were extraordinarily beautiful.And he was amazed by what he read, stunning women prepared to exchange time and intimacy for cash and security with an older and rich man.The number of attractive women was endless. And as he scrolled through the profiles, he couldn't believe just how many options a richer and older man had to choose room.One profile caught his eyes........but it wasn't the tagline that stopped him in

---

1. https://books2read.com/u/mV6XPp

2. https://books2read.com/u/mV6XPp

his tracks........Bored housewife seeking rich man for no strings attached intimacy!It was the fact that the woman looked very much like his wife.*And in fact, on closer inspection - the curious husband was certain the profile belonged to his wife.* **What would you do if you found your wife on a Sugar Dating website?** *This scorching hot novel is part 1 of the series 'Hotwife Sugar' and features adultery, a cheating wife and a husband refusing to believe the rumours and the hard evidence of his wife playing away from home*

About the Author

Sign up to my mailing list to receive the two free epilogues for 'A Hotwife Adventure' and 'Hotwife Training' and to stay up to date on all of my latest releases! http://eepurl.com/c3ICWf Sign up to my Patreon account and receive exclusive Hotwife stories every month and sexy scenes every week! https://www.patreon.com/karlyviolet

Read more at https://www.patreon.com/karlyviolet.

About the Publisher